TOO LATE

By Eleanor Robins

Development: Kent Publishing Services, Inc.
Design and Production: Signature Design Group, Inc.
Illustrations: Jan Naimo Jones

SADDLEBACK PUBLISHING, INC.
Three Watson
Irvine, CA 92618-2767

E-Mail: info@sdlback.com
Website: www.sdlback.com

ISBN 1-56254-693-7

Printed in the United States of America

1 2 3 4 5 6 08 07 06 05 04 03

Chapter 1

Matt was at his locker. Troy was at his locker too. Troy was Matt's best friend. And Troy's locker was next to Matt's locker.

"Do you have a date for Friday night?" Troy asked.

"No. But I am going to ask Sue," Matt said.

Matt had been dating Sue for about six weeks.

Troy said, "You had better ask her soon. I already have a date. So maybe we can all do something together."

"I see Sue at her locker. I will go ask her now," Matt said.

Sue's locker was across the hall from their lockers.

Troy said, "Don't do it now. Do it later. You need to get to class. Or you will be late."

"I have time," Matt said.

Matt got his history book out of his locker.

Troy hurried off to class.

Matt went over to Sue. He said, "Want to go out Friday night?"

Sue said, "Sure. What time will you be over?"

"Is 7:30 OK?" Matt asked.

"Sure. Where do you want to go?" Sue asked.

The warning bell rang.

Sue said, "Tell me later. I have to go to class."

Matt said, "OK. I will call you after baseball practice. And we can talk about what we want to do."

Matt was on the baseball team. He was one of the pitchers.

Sue's class was near their lockers. So Sue hurried into her classroom.

Matt's class was on the other side of the school. There was no way he would get to class on time.

Matt started to his class. The late bell rang. But he didn't worry about it. He wasn't in a hurry to get to class.

Matt didn't like history. And he was already late. So a few more minutes would not matter. And it was only his first time to be late.

The door to his class was closed. He opened the door and went in. Class had already started. Miss Brent always started class on time.

All of the other students looked at him.

Matt went to his desk and sat down.

Miss Brent stopped what she was doing. She said, "You know the class rules, Matt. Be on time. Or plan to stay after school for 30 minutes."

How could he not know the class rules? Miss Brent had them on the inside of the door. Be late more than one time. And you had to stay after school for 30 minutes. And work on history.

Matt said, "It is only my first time. I don't have to stay the first time."

Miss Brent said, "Don't be late again. We don't have time to waste in this class. And we don't have time to hear how many times you have been late. And for me to tell you what we are doing."

What was the big deal? Matt could ask Ed what they were doing. Ed sat in front of him. Ed made the best grades. And Ed always knew everything.

It was not a big deal to be late to class. But Miss Brent had to make it one. She couldn't just let him walk in late. She had to stop the class to say something to him.

Why did he have to have Miss Brent? Some days he had been late to his first semester class. But that teacher did not start class on time. So she didn't care that he was a few minutes late.

Chapter 2

Matt was glad when class was over. It had seemed like the class would never end.

He hurried out of the room. He had PE next. And he didn't want to be late.

Coach Karr was the teacher. He was also the baseball coach. Troy was in the class too.

Matt hurried to the gym and went in. He got there before most of the class had come.

He saw Troy. He went over to Troy.

Troy said, "I was wrong."

"About what?" Matt asked.

Troy said, "I thought I had a date for

Friday night. But I don't. My date has to go out of town with her parents."

"Too bad. Ask someone else," Matt said.

"I might. But I don't think I will. I have to write a paper for my English class. So I will stay home. And work on it," Troy said.

Matt was glad he didn't have Troy's English teacher.

"Are you going to work on your paper all weekend?" Matt asked.

Troy said, "No. Just Friday night. I still have a date for Saturday night. Did you ask Sue for a date?"

"Yeah," Matt said.

"What did she say?" Troy asked.

Matt said, "She said yes. I have to call her later about where we are going. The warning bell rang. So she had to get to class."

"You must have been late to class," Troy said.

"I was," Matt said.

"I told you that you would be," Troy said.

"I know. But I wanted to talk to Sue," Matt said.

"How late were you?" Troy asked.

Matt said, "Only a few minutes. But Miss Brent made a big deal out of it."

Troy said, "She starts class on time. That's why she made a big deal because you were late."

"She should wait a few minutes before she starts. To give us time to get there," Matt said.

"Why? Are a lot of kids late to her class?" Troy asked.

Matt said, "No. I was the first one to be late."

Troy said, "You better not be late

again. Or you will have to stay after school. And then you will be late to baseball practice."

Coach Karr blew his whistle. So the boys had to stop talking.

Chapter 3

It was Friday night. It was a few minutes after eight. Matt had just gotten to Sue's house.

Matt could see Sue. She was looking out the window. Matt started to walk to the front door. But he did not hurry.

Sue opened the door before he got to it.

Sue said, "Are you OK? I was worried about you."

"Why?" Matt asked.

"You are 30 minutes late," Sue said.

Matt said, "Why were you worried? I have been late before."

"But only by five or ten minutes," Sue said.

"Well, I am here now. Are you ready to go?" Matt said.

"Am I ready to go? I have been ready for 30 minutes. Why were you so late?" Sue said.

"I had to do something with Troy after practice. It took longer than I thought it would. And I got home late," Matt said.

"You should have called," Sue said.

"You knew I was coming over here. So why should I call?" Matt said.

"To tell me you would be late," Sue said.

"Why? I was only 30 minutes late," Matt said.

"Why? Because I have been sitting around here waiting for you," Sue said. She seemed to be mad.

Matt didn't say anything. He thought Sue was making a big deal out of nothing.

"Don't you have anything to say?" Sue asked.

"About what?" Matt asked.

"You don't seem to care you were late. And that I had to wait so long," Sue said.

"It is not that big a deal," Matt said.

Matt could see that he had said the wrong thing.

Sue said, "Maybe not to you. But it is to me. Be late again without calling. And I won't date you anymore."

"You don't mean that," Matt said.

"Yes, I do," Sue said.

Matt didn't think she meant it. But he would say he was sorry so they could go.

"I am sorry I was late, Sue. And I won't be late again," Matt said.

"You better not be. Or it is over for us," Sue said.

Matt didn't like what Sue said. But he was not worried. Sue liked him. She would not stop going out with him just because he was late.

Chapter 4

It was the next week. It was the day before Carter High's first baseball game with Hillman. Matt hoped he would be the starting pitcher.

Carter High had already played two games and won. But Zack had been the starting pitcher.

Matt had been working hard. He would find out today who the starting pitcher would be. And Coach Karr had said it might be Matt.

Matt was on his way to the gym to see Coach Karr. He saw Troy in the hall.

Troy called to him. He said, "Your class isn't that way. Where are you going?"

Matt said, "To the gym. To find out who the starting pitcher will be. Coach Karr said he would tell me."

"You don't have time to do that now. Ask him at PE," Troy said.

"But I want to know now. I don't want to wait," Matt said.

"You will be late to Miss Brent's class. And have to stay after school. And be late to practice," Troy said.

"The coach will write me a late pass," Matt said.

"Don't be too sure of that. But do what you want to do. And I know you will. Good luck," Troy said.

"Thanks. See you in PE," Matt said.

Matt went quickly to the gym. Coach Karr's PE class was already there.

Matt saw Coach Karr. He was talking to Zack. Zack was in his PE class.

Matt had to wait to talk to Coach Karr.

Then the coach saw Matt. He said, "What are you doing here, Matt?"

Matt said, "Who will be the starting pitcher? You said you would tell me this morning."

"We don't have time to talk right now, Matt. It is almost time for my class to start. We can talk at your PE time. You need to get to your class," Coach Karr said.

Then Coach Karr started to talk to Zack again.

Was he telling Zack that Zack would be the starting pitcher?

Matt was sure Coach Karr wasn't telling Zack that. Matt was sure he would be the starting pitcher.

Matt hurried out of the gym. He heard the warning bell. He walked quickly down the hall.

Then he heard the late bell. He was going to be late again.

Miss Brent would be sure to make a big deal about it. And tell him he would have to stay after school.

Matt opened the door to his class and went in. Miss Brent stopped teaching and looked at him. All of the other students looked at him too.

"Matt, plan to stay after school Monday," Miss Brent said.

"I can't stay Monday. I have baseball practice," Matt said.

"You know the class rules, Matt," Miss Brent said.

Matt said, "I had to go to the gym. Coach Karr needed to see me."

That was almost true. But Matt was the one who needed to see Coach Karr. Coach Karr didn't need to see him.

"We don't have time to hear why you were late. Stay after class. You need to get your after school slip," Miss Brent said.

Matt wasn't worried. He was sure Coach Karr would give him a late pass. Then Miss Brent would not make him stay. But he would still have to talk to her after class.

Matt did not like history. And he didn't want to be in Miss Brent's class. So he was glad when the class was over.

Matt went to talk to Miss Brent. She was writing an after school slip for him.

"You don't need to do that," Matt said.

Miss Brent looked up at him. She looked surprised. She said, "Why not?"

"Coach Karr will write me a late pass. I can bring it to you after school," Matt said.

"Why do you think he will do that?" Miss Brent asked.

"I told you when I came late. Coach Karr needed to see me," Matt said.

"Why didn't he send a pass with you?" Miss Brent asked.

"He didn't have time to write one. A boy in his PE class needed to talk to him," Matt said.

Matt hoped Miss Brent would say he could go. And come back after school. But she didn't.

She wrote some more on the after school slip. Then she handed it to Matt.

She said, "Here is your after school slip. Plan to stay Monday. Unless Coach Karr does give you a late pass."

She didn't look like she thought Coach Karr would.

But Matt was sure he would.

Chapter 5

Matt hurried to PE as quickly as he could. He was almost late.

He saw Troy as he walked into the gym.

"Did you find out?" Troy asked.

Matt said, "No. Coach Karr didn't have time to talk. I am going to ask him now. And I have to get a late pass."

"For Miss Brent?" Troy asked.

Matt said, "Yeah. She said I have to stay after school Monday."

"Are you sure the coach will give you a late pass?" Troy asked.

"Why wouldn't he? I was here talking to him," Matt said.

"I wouldn't count on it," Troy said.

But Matt was sure the coach would give him a late pass. He would not want Matt to be late to practice.

Matt hurried over to Coach Karr. He had to know who the starting pitcher would be before class started.

Matt said, "Who is going to start the Hillman game?"

"Zack," Coach Karr said.

Matt had been sure he would be the starting pitcher.

Coach Karr said, "We play Hillman again next week. Work hard. And maybe you will be ready to start that game."

But Matt would not be able to work that hard Monday. Unless the coach gave him a late pass.

Matt said, "I need a late pass."

Coach Karr looked surprised. He said, "Why?"

"I was late to Miss Brent's class," Matt said.

"Why do you think I should give you a late pass?" Coach Karr asked.

"Because I came to talk to you. That is why I was late," Matt said.

Coach Karr said, "I can't give you a late pass, Matt. I didn't tell you to come talk to me. You came on your own."

"But Miss Brent said I have to stay after school Monday. And I will be late to practice," Matt said.

"Why do you have to stay after school?" Coach Karr asked.

Matt said, "It is one of her rules. Be late to class more than one time. And you have to stay after school for 30 minutes."

"Did you know about this rule

before today?" Coach Karr asked.

Matt said, "Yeah. She told us the first day. And she has her rules on the door."

Coach Karr did not look pleased. He said, "You knew you might be late. And have to stay after school. But you still came to talk to me."

"I wanted to know who the starting pitcher would be. And I knew you would write me a late pass," Matt said.

"But you came on your own, Matt. So you will have to stay Monday. But don't be late again to my practice," Coach Karr said.

Two boys came over to talk to the coach. So Matt walked over to Troy.

"Are you going to start?" Troy asked.

Matt said, "No. Zack is. But we play Hillman again next week. Coach Karr said work hard. And I might be ready to start that game."

"Did you tell him about Monday?" Troy asked.

"Yeah," Matt said.

"Did he say he would give you a late pass?" Troy asked.

Matt said, "No. But maybe I will not have to stay. Maybe I can get Miss Brent to let me out of it."

"Don't count on it," Troy said.

But Matt hoped he could.

Matt stopped by his locker before his last class. Troy was at his locker too.

Matt got all the books he needed for his homework.

"Why are you getting all those books now?" Troy asked.

"I have to talk to Miss Brent after school. I don't have time to go to my locker. And talk to her. And get to practice on time," Matt said.

Troy said, "Good luck. But I think she will still make you stay Monday."

Matt hoped Troy was wrong.

Matt thought his last class would never end. He was in a hurry to see Miss Brent.

He was glad when the class was over.

Matt hurried to Miss Brent's room. He was glad no students were still there.

Miss Brent was at her desk. She was grading papers. She looked up when Matt walked over to her desk.

"Did Coach Karr give you a late pass?" she asked.

"No, he didn't," Matt said.

"Then why are you here?" Miss Brent asked.

"I can't stay after school Monday," Matt said.

"You know the rules, Matt," Miss Brent said.

"But I can't stay Monday. I have baseball practice. And I can't be late to it," Matt said.

Miss Brent did not look pleased. She said, "So you think it is OK to be late to my class. But not to baseball practice."

"I didn't say that," Matt said. But that was what he thought.

"I will see you Monday after school," Miss Brent said.

Matt wanted to say more. But he knew he had already said too much.

Chapter 6

It was Friday night. Matt had to go to the store for his mom. So he was late getting to Sue's house.

But he wasn't 30 minutes late this time. He was only 20 minutes late.

He thought Sue might be looking out the window. But she wasn't.

Matt walked up to the front door. He rang the bell. But Sue didn't come to the door. He rang the bell again. Sue opened the door.

Sue didn't look glad to see him. She said, "You are late again."

Matt said, "I know. But I had to do something for my mom."

Matt smiled at Sue. But she did not smile back.

She didn't move so Matt could go in the house. So he said, "Are you ready to go?"

"No," Sue said.

She just stood there.

Did she plan for him to stand on her front porch all night?

"Are you going to let me in?" Matt asked.

Sue opened the door more so Matt could come in. Then she closed the door. She stayed next to the door. She didn't say anything.

Matt and Sue just looked at each other for a few minutes.

Then Matt said, "I'm sorry I was late."

At first Sue just looked at Matt.

Then she said, "You aren't just late. You are too late. You don't care about me. And about how I feel."

That surprised Matt. He said, "Why did you say that?"

"You are 20 minutes late," Sue said.

"But I am doing better. I was 30 minutes late last time," Matt said.

"You just don't get it," Sue said.

Matt said, "Yes, I do. But I was only late. Don't make a big deal out of it. I was helping my mom. It's not like I was with some other girl."

Sue didn't say anything.

"Do you want to sit down and talk about this?" Matt said.

He didn't want to talk about it any more. But maybe Sue did.

Sue said, "Why? I told you how I felt last time. Be late again without calling. And it was over for us. You were late. You didn't call. So it is over for us."

That surprised Matt.

"You don't mean that," he said.

But Sue did look like she did.

She said, "Yes, I do. It is over for us, Matt."

She opened the door. So Matt knew she wanted him to go. That made Matt mad. She was not being fair.

Matt said, "Fine with me. You aren't the only girl in the world."

But she was the only girl he wanted to date.

Matt left Sue's house. And he went home. He called Troy as soon as he got home.

Troy said, "Where are you?"

"At home," Matt said.

"Why aren't you with Sue?" Troy asked.

"She broke up with me," Matt said.

"Why?" Troy asked.

"Because I was late. She said I didn't care about her. Just because I was late. And I didn't call," Matt said.

Troy said, "Why didn't you call Sue? Didn't you know you would be late?"

"It wasn't a big deal. It was only 20 minutes. Would you have called?" Matt said.

Troy said, "Sure. But I am not like you. I try to be on time. You don't. You have a problem about being late."

That surprised Matt. He said, "I don't have a problem about being late."

Troy said, "Yes, you do. You are late to class. And late for dates. But you don't seem to care. Unless you have to stay after school. Or a girl gets upset with you."

Matt said, "That is not true. You

sound just like Miss Brent and Sue."

He didn't have a problem about being late. And he was sorry he called Troy. He didn't want to talk to Troy any longer.

"I have to go. I will see you Monday," Matt said.

First Miss Brent. Then Sue. And now Troy. They were the ones with a problem about time. Not Matt.

Chapter 7

It was Monday morning. Matt saw Sue at her locker before school. He walked over to her. Maybe she wasn't mad at him anymore.

"Hi, Sue," he said.

She slammed her locker shut and walked off.

Troy walked up to Matt.

"Sue must still be mad at you," Troy said.

Matt said, "No big deal. There are a lot of other girls in the world."

He just wished he wanted to date them.

But Sue would get over being mad at

him. And then she could try to talk to him. And maybe he wouldn't talk to her. For a day or two.

Matt's day had gotten off to a bad start.

And the day went slowly for Matt. But he was glad.

He was in no hurry to stay after school for Miss Brent.

But he did hurry to Miss Brent's class as soon as school was over. He wanted his 30 minutes to start. So he could get them over. And he could go to baseball practice.

Matt sat down and started to do his work. But he kept looking at the clock.

He worked for 30 minutes. Then he said, "My 30 minutes are up, Miss Brent. Can I go?"

"Yes, Matt. And don't be late again," Miss Brent said.

Matt left Miss Brent's class. And he hurried to practice. He worked as hard as he could.

And he worked hard the next three afternoons.

It was Thursday. And it was almost time for practice to be over. The Hillman game was the next day. Matt wanted to know who the starting pitcher would be. But he did not want to ask Coach Karr.

Coach Karr called Zack over. Matt could not hear what he said to Zack.

Then Zack ran over to one of the catchers. He started throwing a ball to the catcher.

Zack did not look happy. So Matt didn't think Zack would be the starting pitcher.

Zack had lost the Hillman game. So Matt thought the coach might let him start. And not Zack. But he was not sure.

Then Coach Karr said, "Matt, I need to see you."

Matt hurried over to Coach Karr. He hoped the coach would say he would be the starting pitcher.

Coach Karr said, "Matt, you have pitched well this week. I want you to start the Hillman game."

"Thanks," Matt said.

"You don't need to thank me, Matt. You are a good pitcher. And you have worked hard this week. Hillman has beat us one time. And they will be hard to beat this time. But I think you can do it," Coach Karr said.

Matt knew they would be hard to beat. But he thought he could beat them too.

Matt said, "I can beat them, Coach.

I am sure of it."

Coach Karr said, "Good. Keep working hard. And keep thinking that you can beat them."

"I will, Coach," Matt said.

Coach Karr said, "And get a lot of rest tonight, Matt. And be ready to pitch your best tomorrow."

"I will, Coach. I can hardly wait," Matt said.

It would be his first time to be the starting pitcher.

Matt could hardly wait to tell Troy the news. He hurried over to Troy.

Troy said, "What did the coach say? You look like it was very good news."

"I will be the starting pitcher in the Hillman game," Matt said.

Troy said, "Way to go. Zack is a good pitcher. But I don't think he can beat them. But I think you can."

Matt said, "I think I can too. But I wasn't sure the coach would let me start. I thought he would pick Zack again."

Troy said, "I am not surprised. You pitch a lot better than you did."

Matt wanted to share his big news with Sue. But she still would not talk to him. Just because he was a few minutes late.

Coach Karr blew his whistle. All of the boys ran over to him.

Coach Karr said, "The Hillman game is an away game. And we can't get there late. Bring everything you need with you to the gym. The bus will leave at 3:10. And I mean 3:10. Be late even a minute or two. And I will leave without you."

Chapter 8

The next day Matt had to stay after science class. He had a test Monday. And he needed to ask Mr. Reese about the test. Mr. Reese was his science teacher.

Matt picked up his notebook. He went over to Mr. Reese. He left his science book on his desk.

Matt found out what he needed to know. Then he quickly left.

He had Miss Brent next. And he could not be late to her class.

The school day went by too slowly for Matt. He was in a hurry to pitch. He was sure he could beat Hillman.

Matt was glad when school was over

for the day. He went to his locker. He got what he needed out of his locker. Then he hurried to the gym.

He put on his uniform as quickly as he could. He could hardly wait to leave for the Hillman game.

Troy said, "I wish we didn't have a science test Monday. Call me when you get home. I need some help with my science."

Matt and Troy both had Mr. Reese for science. But not at the same time. And they had the same work to do.

Matt looked for his science book. He didn't see it.

"I thought I got all of the books I needed. But I must have left my science book in my locker. I have to go get it," Matt said.

Troy said, "You better tell Coach Karr. I don't think you have time to get it. And I don't think Coach Karr will wait for you."

Matt said, "Sure he will. I have to have my book to study. And only the gym will be open when we get back."

Matt hurried over to Coach Karr. He told the coach what he needed to do and why.

Coach Karr did not look pleased. He said, "You should have had all your books when you came to the gym. I told all of you boys that yesterday. Didn't you hear me say that?"

"Yes," Matt said.

Coach Karr said, "Go get your book. You need it to study. But you need to know one thing."

"What?" Matt asked.

"We leave at 3:10. I told all of you that yesterday too. You have to get your book. But I don't have to wait for you.

Be back before 3:10. Or I will leave without you," Coach Karr said.

"I will be back before then," Matt said.

He was sure he could get to his locker and back before then.

Matt hurried to his locker. But his book was not there.

Where could it be?

He had been in a hurry to leave science. So he would not be late to Miss Brent's class. He must have left his book in his science class.

Did he have time to go get it?

Matt wasn't sure. But he was not worried. He was the starting pitcher. There was no way the coach would leave without him.

Matt hurried to his science class.

Mr. Reese said, "What are you doing

here, Matt? It is time for you to leave for the game."

Matt said, "I left my book in here."

Matt looked in his desk. But his book was not there.

"Look on the back table," Mr. Reese said.

Matt hurried to the table. He found his book.

Matt looked up at the school clock. It was already 3:10.

He hurried back to the gym as fast as he could go. But he was sure Coach Karr would wait for him.

He hurried into the gym.

He didn't see Coach Karr or any of the team.

Matt ran outside.

He saw the team bus going down the school drive. But it was too late for him to catch up with it.

He was too late. And the coach had left him.

First Miss Brent. Then Sue. Then Troy. And now Coach Karr. They didn't think it was OK for him to be late.

Maybe he was the one with the problem about time. And not all of them.

He had to quit being late. And he had to get to places on time.

Matt hoped Carter High would win the game. But Carter High lost. Maybe because he did not pitch.

Matt hoped Coach Karr would give him another chance to pitch. But he did not know if Coach Karr would.

But one thing he did know. The next time he would not be late.